Metaphor's Miracle

Dalian Graylocke

ISBN-13: 978-0692605684
ISBN-10: 0692605681

Written by Dalian Graylocke
https://www.facebook.com/DalianGraylockeOfficial/

Edited & Prepared for Publication by Jennifer-Crystal Johnson
www.JenniferCrystalJohnson.com

This short story is a part of the Metaphor series by Dalian Graylocke, but intended for the Christmas season as a standalone piece.

Special thanks to my beloved
David Kaiser
for showing me what real love looks like.

Other Books by Dalian Graylocke

Metaphor, Broken Publications January 2016

The World as I Know It

The world I live in is probably different from yours. Quite a few years ago, a scientist named Dr. Erik Graham discovered a compound that unlocked human potential. At least that's what they preferred to call it, but I'm not really sure anymore.

It works like this: everyone has a special energy that is somehow connected to the world around them. This energy was called *Auros* by Dr. Graham. The human *Auros* also has the ability to heal the body, and so Dr. Graham sold the patent for his compound, called *Genaurosfacili-A* or what we commonly call packets, to a research hospital called ANGEL. The hospital manufactured the packets in the hopes that it would cure cancer and that's just the weirdest part. The packet worked, but it had a really serious defect that made it unusable for the general public, which is why you probably have never heard about it.

It unlocked the *Auros'* true power. This made the feds come in and create an organization within the hospital to regulate the poor individuals whose genes mutated and allowed them to use what you might understand as super powers.

There are currently two kinds of powered individuals, which we call Chosen, and those are the first generations and the second generations. The first generations are the people who were unlucky enough to have consumed a packet, usually by force or illegal means.

The second gens are just what they sound like: the children of the first gens.

I'm actually a first generation despite my relatively young age. My mother illegally managed to get a packet and took it while she was pregnant with me. The result ended up aborting me, but because of my *Auros* being activated, my DNA latched on to some kind of plant source so I could survive outside of my mother's womb.

The end result of that is that I have strange, gray skin because of the chlorophyll inside of me. The upside to my 'defect' is that it makes me a bit more adaptable than most other humans. It also makes me slightly... inhuman, I suppose. Or superhuman might work, too. I have only ever been sick twice in my life; the first time left me with a vein-like scar on my left cheek and the second caused my appendix to contain too much of what turned out to be a beneficial-to-others bacteria, so I had to have it removed.

My biological father was unable to take care of me when I was an infant, so I was taken in by a good friend of his, a woman named Michal. She married into a very prominent family: the Graham family. Yes, those Grahams.

They took care of me until I was about four years old, which was when I got sick the second time. My father took me in after that. That was when my life became hell.

I won't go into too much detail, but suffice it to say that I was trained to be a soldier. The government branch that presides over us Chosen needed specialized people that could hunt down our own kind who break the law or use their *Auros* for their own gains, a group we call RUCs, pronounced 'rooks.' Those of us who are registered with ANGEL are called ARCs, pronounced 'arks.'

Anyone who breaks the laws designed specifically for us Chosen are called Rogues.

That's probably all you really need to know about Chosen.

I was trained to be focused on my missions. If I didn't have one, I was training for one. This was my whole life until I was about ten years old.

That was when I met *her*.

If I had been adopted by the Graham family, she would have been my sister, but I'm glad it worked out differently. I like my father well enough, and I admire Michal like a mother, but *she* is probably the only person in my life that I've ever felt this way for.

Rachel.

She's four and a half years my junior, but she always seemed far more grown up than even most of the adults I know. She's a beautiful girl, with one blue eye and one hazel green, and her hair looks like she started curling it in tight cascades and stopped only at the top, the rest of it having a gentle wave. Her skin is pale and peppered with light freckles and her hair is a deep auburn red.

She is also an enigma like me; she is what is known as a chimera. She is the daughter of two fathers and her mother, Michal. She merged with her fraternal twin sister in the womb, but I think her unusual qualities make her even more beautiful.

Her family is a little mixed up. I don't know all the details, but Michal married Adam Graham and had been with him for four years when something very bad happened. Adam's older brother, Shane, took care of her when Adam disappeared and she remarried him. Five years later, Adam returned with a child of his own from some illicit relationship he'd had when he was away.

All I know is that during those five years, Adam wasn't himself. He had since tried to be a father to the children he left behind, and to Rachel. They're all used to it now, but it was a serious adjustment, especially for Adam, codenamed Savior, who had to get used to the fact that his wife was now married to his brother.

Probably the last thing you should know about the Graham family is that Michal and Shane share a very special bond that doesn't exist in any other Chosen. Their bond allows them to hear each other's surface thoughts and communicate telepathically. Since their *Auros* are bound to each other, they can use each other's *Auros*. Shane can also sense how his children are feeling, which is really convenient for him.

Shane is someone to really look up to. He's relaxed and a total family man. He's understanding, or at least tries to be, even though he had a really terrible childhood. It was because his father wasn't a very good man, from what I understand. Michal is a loving and doting mother, and she's very empathetic to others. Together, Shane and Michal are an amazing team and are well liked at ANGEL for all the good they do.

When I was sixteen and had worked up my courage to tell eleven-year-old Rachel how I felt about her, a bond similar to her parents' formed between us, and they were the only ones who could really understand what happened and what we were going through.

It was awkward at first because they had assumed sex was involved. I only kissed her and told her that I was in love with her, and she told me she loved me, too. I felt her then, her immense, complicated feelings for me, and her confused thoughts that popped into my head like they were my own, but in her voice.

We are still trying to figure it all out, but I found that I could use only some of her *Auros*, while she could use all of mine, and I can hear her thoughts, but she can't hear mine yet. It changes as we grow older, but the constant is that I can feel her feelings and she can feel mine.

This is a blessing and a curse.

I recently turned 18, but I'm lucky. I'll spare the details, but I almost died last year. Rachel was driven close to insane when she felt me slipping away. I've felt bad about that, and since then, it physically hurts her to be away from me for too long. It was explained to me that our bond – or tether, as some call it – frayed and couldn't be stretched as far as it used to.

This led to me being given permission by her parents to move in. Adam didn't like it at all, but they had an apartment on the grounds for me which is separate from the main house, and I'm not allowed to be strictly alone with her... but it's nice to ease her anxiety when I've been working for too long.

To be honest, it's a huge relief for me to be able to be with her after a long day. My job includes a lot of detective work. I see a lot of things, from uncontrolled abilities to dead bodies. Some people find this fact horrific, but this has been my life since I could remember. I tend to come home from work a little tense, and she relaxes me. I love to smell her auburn hair and run my fingers through it. We'll talk, but it's mostly just to hear each other's voices. We can sit in complete silence and be perfectly happy, but I'd rather hear her talk about her day than glean it from using our bond.

I'm a commander of a group of teens about my age. My best friend is Sherlock Basset, a half-man half-dog with a keen sense of smell and a deep love for me. It may or may not be what you're thinking, though.

To explain this, I have to explain that Sherlock is at odds with his own emotions every day of his life. As a hound, he feels everything quite deeply, but as a young man a year and a half my junior, he can't quite decipher what he's feeling. Usually he's a happy-go-lucky type. As for his feelings for me, it's about the same as a dog who adopts just one person. That person is *his* person. He will obey this person no matter what and wants to be with this person every waking moment of every day.

I am his person. I'm like his 'master,' I suppose, but I'm not. Sherlock has his own mind and it's a very keen and interesting one; smart and sly. I have no problems calling him my number one because I know I can trust him with my life. He might feel more strongly for me than I do him, but I care deeply about him. He's like a brother to me, and I'm glad I have at least one person in this world that I can trust like that.

As for the other members of my unit, I only have three others under me: Daniel Torres, Sylvia Stern, and Terra Grayson. Daniel is the kind of person who cares deeply about doing a good job, but he doesn't always take everything into account, which is an obvious problem. Terra is a sweetheart and generally just does the secretarial stuff, but Sylvia is the biggest pain in my ass. She doesn't like to listen to me no matter what I say and has found herself in ANGEL's prison cell (known as The Tank) more than once because of it.

I'm writing this down because I have a story I want to immortalize. I want to remember every detail of this Christmas, so

I ask that you bear with me as I write down my memories of the one time I saw a miracle with my own eyes.

Fireside Conversations

Being part plant has unexpected benefits, and one of these is the fact that I'm not bothered by the cold. It was December 20th and I was still carrying that damn box in my coat pocket like it was some kind of life line.

After the events of last year, I sort of felt like a stranger in my own body. I had found out why just that day, actually, and now I had to tell Rachel and I wasn't looking forward to it. I still needed to give her the gift I had meant to give her last year, and now this piece of news seemed far more important.

Even more pressing, however, was the fact that I was late getting out of work. I looked up at the deep gray sky as large, feather-like snowflakes gently drifted down, annoyingly collecting on the streets and making driving a hazard, unless you were used to it because you were from Colorado Springs.

I got into my car – a sleek, black Mustang GT that my father got me for my 15th birthday when I was emancipated and became an 'adult.' I sighed and listened to the stylings of orchestral pop music as I drove as quickly but as carefully as I could. It was slick, but thankfully not terrible by Colorado standards, which I suppose could be saying something about how crazy drivers are out here. I watched a truck almost spin out in front of me as it tried to garner traction on the fresh snow.

I breathed a sigh of relief when I arrived at home and locked my car, its locking chirp reverberating off of walls like an emergency siren. I made my way around the back of the house where I knew she was and gently slid open the glass doors of the two story Victorian home.

I found my love lazily laying on the couch by the fireplace in the living room. For a moment, I admired her before I climbed over the back of the couch and slid behind her, her tiny body fitting comfortably between my legs. I held her close, kissed her head, and flexed my fingers through her hair, admiring how beautiful her young face was.

Almost fourteen. The love of my life was only thirteen. I twisted my lips as I silently contemplated that thought when she stretched and twisted around, clasping her arms around my neck and shoulders and looking up at me with those beautiful mismatched eyes.

"Welcome home, Timothy," she murmured softly. I was so in love with her and took a moment to nervously kiss her lips, pulling aside her auburn curtain of hair. I wanted to give my gift to her. She deserved to have it, but I also needed to tell her—

We were interrupted by Adam marching through the room with a newspaper in one hand and his brows knit together in a hard, admonishing gaze aimed at me.

"You do know that there's a front door, don't you?" he growled at me, sitting down in one of the overstuffed chairs in the living room.

I didn't bat an eye as I promptly replied, "Yes, sir."

Rachel gazed up at me, her voice in my head telling me that she thought my tone was a little disrespectful, though she knew I hadn't meant it that way.

I got irritated with Adam for treating me like some kind of interloper who wanted to steal his daughter's innocence. Well, maybe I did, but I held it back. I could definitely wait for her. She was well worth the wait, and I enjoyed just cuddling with her on that plush couch. I knew there were boundaries for having such a young girlfriend, and I never forgot them. I wished he would have just trusted me, but he never really seemed to.

"You might want to try using it next time," Adam warned.

"Papa Adam...." Rachel complained, gazing at him from my shoulder. Adam glanced at her with some unreadable expression on his face.

"Hey, Tim-o! When did you get in?" Shane said as he came into the room with a gigantic smile on his face. I never understood how he could be so jovial all the time, but I always felt like I could really relax with him around.

"Just now, sir," I replied, used to giving curt answers.

"I still don't understand why he's even here," Adam remarked, noisily opening his paper. I didn't think for one second that he read any of it. It was Adam's way of guarding his daughter from me and keeping an eye on our interactions.

I'm sure if they knew what happened when they were in bed, they'd definitely disapprove.

"Timothy and Rachel are Silver Cord tethered, so they have to have a certain amount of physical contact or it literally hurts them," Shane explained, his tone a little irritated.

"I don't like all the time he spends with my daughter," Adam grumbled and I felt Rachel clutch my shirt and grit her teeth as Adam called her *his*. She hated it.

I decided to try to shift the focus back onto me. "I apologize and will announce that I'm home from now on."

Adam's response was to glare at me coldly before returning his attention to his newspaper. Shane offered me a slight smile, his dark, curly hair falling over his brow as he shifted his gaze to the ceiling, looking altogether drained.

"Hard case at work?" I asked him.

It was Adam who responded as he noisily turned a page of his paper. "Absolutely nothing to do with a kid like you," he said gruffly.

"I'd like to remind you that I'm eighteen, sir," I shot back, a little more than annoyed now.

"Which is exactly why you're dating my thirteen-year-old daughter?" he asked, folding his paper in his lap. I stared, unable to help myself. Why couldn't he just understand? Why did he feel the need to impose his beliefs onto Rachel, who — as far as she was concerned — only shared some of his DNA?

Shane intervened. "Whew, little bro, who's on the rag today?" he asked, shifting and leaning forward in his chair.

Adam's expression darkened dangerously, but Shane remained cheerful.

"Ease up on the kid, will you? You liked him well enough, back in the day. Don't forget that every single day of his life before the bond formed, Timothy was dutifully looking out for Babydoll without even being asked. She has yet to come to harm and people have seriously tried. Do you honestly think that a boy who almost died—" he caught himself too late and Rachel's fingernails dug into my shoulder as she held on tight, holding her breath.

"I get your point. I'm sorry, I guess. But I remember being that young—" Shane cut in again.

"You never stopped being that young."

I laughed softly, unable to help myself. Adam's *Auros* was of the healing variety, which – to people like Rachel who could actually see *Auros* – was the color pink. His healing abilities made him a rare thing so far in terms of the Chosen. He was what we called a *regener,* meaning that he wouldn't grow old, could heal quickly, and it seemed as if he couldn't be killed. Adam was, so far, permanently twenty years old.

The reminder of my near-death experience shocked me and Rachel sat up, looking down at me wide-eyed.

"What's wrong, Tim?" she asked, tucking her gracefully long hair behind her ear. I gazed up at her, trying to control my nerves. I took down killers, criminals, and general bad guys with powers, so why should this be so hard?

"I...." I began, but Rachel's sisters suddenly started squealing as they ran into the fire-lit living room, jumping onto Shane's lap.

"Baby girls!" Shane cried, hugging them happily.

The oldest one was a pretty cute carbon copy of her father, Adam, but with slightly curly light blonde hair. Her eyes were wide and blue and she had an athletic build that seemed to be common in the Graham family. Her name was Raye Addison-Graham, and she was the child Adam brought with him when he suddenly returned after his years-long absence.

The other was a beautiful mix of her parents, with Shane's curly hair, Michal's face, hazel green eyes, and her father's personality, which from what I could tell, drove Shane insane. She was Charlotte Graham, but everyone called her Charlie. They were eleven and eight, respectively.

"Daddy, I want a doll for Christmas!" Charlie cried with so much innocent joy in her tone, it kind of hurt. I couldn't remember a time I ever felt like that. Rachel responded to the sad feeling by kissing my cheek lovingly. I smiled at her.

"Uncle Shane, I want a unicorn!" Raye announced.

Shane groaned, smiling. "Oh, no... not the one that's being blasted all over the TV right now!"

I watched the exchange with some interest, seeing as I only ever experienced that kind of joy at Christmas when I was being fostered by Adam and Michal. My father celebrated with me, but he'd never asked me about stuff I wanted, and Christmas was more like a trip to Waffle House where he'd slip me whatever present he happened to get me that year. I think the first gift my father ever gave me were cookies that I couldn't eat because I can't digest animal protein.

Dad later joked about how I couldn't have been descended from a Venus flytrap. I really learned to hate that joke. As if my gray skin wasn't enough to make me self-conscious....

The most useful of Dad's presents was a multi-tool and textbook for paramedics that I had been interested in, but I digress.

I raised my eyebrow as Rachel's voice sounded off in my head. She was thinking about a Christmas that happened some years back, when she was eight and had wanted to give me something as a token of her appreciation that made me blush. This girl....

She literally got me mint leaves. Freshly picked, if the taste had been any indication. I had no idea where she got them, but it was a fond memory for her. I got the impression that she'd learned how to use her white *Auros* to grow plant life and purchased the seeds at an organic store to grow them herself.

I stared at her now, amazed and touched that she had gone to such lengths. She turned bright red and hugged my arm, pressing her head to my shoulder to hide her face.

"I love you," I whispered. She gave my arm a little squeeze and stopped moving, watching her father tease her sisters.

"What do you want for Christmas, Rachel?" Adam asked suddenly. The room got very quiet and Rachel slowly raised her head. I felt the sting of her sadness as if it were my own. It was painful for her, and I didn't understand why until the words came out of her mouth.

"I want a Christmas party."

I got chills and found myself kneeling before her, holding her hands in mine and gazing up at her, as if prostrating myself like that would somehow protect her from the horrible events that suddenly flashed through her mind.

Last Christmas, I had been careless and it almost cost me my life. Rachel had been hurt more than just emotionally by it, and I wish I could take it back. I realized that my window for telling her was over as she gazed at me tearfully.

"Just the family and close friends, Babydoll?" Shane asked, sitting next to Rachel and taking her into his arms. I understood and got on my feet, backing away. I only stayed long enough to watch her nod miserably before I slipped out the door.

I sighed and stared at the sky as it continued snowing gently before walking over to the guest house apartment that I had been given to stay in.

The guest house of the Graham Estate was far too big for just me. I certainly wasn't used to the space, and the house was designed for a family of four. I'd been told Shane lived there before his first marriage fell apart. I'd heard he set up his ex-wife in a house just next door and she was happy there, even though her health had begun failing in recent years. Shane never failed to visit her at least once a week. What a guy.

I sighed and threw myself down on the couch, flipping on the TV if just for the noise. I didn't want to think. Thinking would lead me to reliving last Christmas, and I would have been happy to forget that day for as long as I lived.

It was one o'clock in the morning when my door opened slowly and Rachel came in, wearing a nightgown straight out of some renaissance movie. I gazed up at her and sighed.

"Hey. I'm sorry—" I began, but she shook her head, her hair neatly plaited into a braid that fell over her left shoulder.

"No, don't be. I'm being stupid, I know," she said, grabbing my wrist and pulling at me.

"It's not stupid, Rachel. Maybe we need to talk about it," I said, letting her pull me off the couch and lead me into the bedroom.

I immediately walked over to the closet and pulled out a tank and pajama bottoms. The room was fairly large with a canopy bed in pastel blues and greens. In the corner, I had set up a screen so I could change when Rachel came over. Rachel sat on the bed and sighed, looking down at her ankles.

"What is there to talk about that hasn't already been said? I woke up from my coma to find you holding me, singing into my hair. We celebrated my birthday instead. You were alive, your wounds had healed, and I was so grateful."

I came out from behind the screen, putting my clothes in a hamper as I passed it and making a beeline for Rachel. I pulled her up into my arms and kissed her. I fell with her onto the bed and, like every night since last Christmas, I held her as she fell asleep, stroking her hair and relishing the heat of her body against mine.

"I felt guilty," I said after a while. Rachel's fingers weaved into my hair and she kissed me.

"Why?" she asked.

I sighed. "Because I felt like I had failed you. That you deserved something better. I'd made a promise to myself that when you woke up, I wouldn't let you see how much our bond screwed with my head. Because you may have felt me slipping away, but I felt you holding on. And it hurt because I didn't want to die more for your sake than mine. That's when I realized that was exactly my problem. I valued your life way above my own, which turns out to be a pretty selfish thing because if I don't take care of myself, how can I be expected to protect you and hold you like this?"

Rachel laughed softly and kissed my nose, which gave me a warm, fuzzy feeling.

"I'm glad you understand," she whispered. I sighed and kissed her neck, holding her hand as I did.

"Hurry and grow the fuck up," I growled at her, knowing that my breath on her neck would give her chills.

"I'm doing the best I can," she laughed and held me extra tight.

Falling asleep in her arms was much like sinking into a warm bath with sunlight on my face. I always woke up feeling refreshed after a full night's rest with her in my arms.

Girl Troubles

The following morning, I ran to the bathroom and then found that Rachel had left me breakfast just the way I liked it, with bread she'd made using just water, yeast, and sprouted seeds.

She was going to make some man a very lucky husband. If only I had the courage to ask her.

Rachel was probably back in her room, getting ready for the special school ANGEL had created for the second gen Chosen, ANGEL Academy. I never attended, but I was a special case anyway.

I had always been proud of my young sweetheart. She was very close to graduating high school. She was following in Adam's footsteps in that particular regard. Adam had graduated from his high school at the age of sixteen; my Rachel was set to do it at the age of fifteen. She was beautiful, smart, and I suppose it didn't help that her *Auros* was white; it was a new color that meant that Rachel had eidetic memory. That was part of what made her learn everything so quickly. She didn't have to bring any books to school; she already had them memorized.

I sighed after I ate and got dressed in my black carpenter jeans and issued ANGEL shirt and jacket with my ID number on it: 00010904. No name, just a number. I supposed it made us harder to identify for the enemy. They couldn't call me by my name, which suited me just fine.

Yesterday had been a waste of good time. I needed to give my present to Rachel, but there just didn't seem to be a right time to do it. I sighed as I fished around in my pocket for the box and felt relieved to find it there.

I was going to try today.

∞

"On the twenty-third?" I asked, a little incredulous as Shane gave me the news. Work had been slow and my best friend and I had just finished our lunch break when Shane joined us.

"Yeah. I'm doing it for Babydoll, so it would be really awesome if you and Sherlie could come," Shane explained, reaching out and ruffling my best friend's hair. Sherlock grinned and closed his black lashes over his light brown eyes, relishing the touch.

"I'll go! I like Rachel," Sherlock said, suddenly scratching an itch on his head with such vigor I was surprised the mutt didn't draw blood.

"You know me," I said, grabbing Sherlock's arm to keep him from hurting himself. Sherlock looked at me in lovesick surprise, his eyes softening. "And stop that. You're going to hurt yourself."

Sherlock grinned at me and 'wagged his tail,' which he didn't actually have. It was more like swaying his hips back and forth, like a dog whose tail had been cut off. I winced at him and the look he was giving me because I knew what was about to happen.

In front of Shane, Sherlock planted a wet one on my cheek and I pushed his head away before the others came.

"Ew, Sherlie! No kisses!" I cried, not really mad. Sherlock instead contented himself to throw his arms around my shoulders and hug me, panting.

Shane laughed and ruffled Sherlock's hair.

"Well, you have to do me a solid and keep this guy from getting himself killed again," he spoke fondly, and a lump formed in my throat.

"Actually, Shane, I—" I began, but was interrupted by Shane's phone going off.

"Shane speaking." He spoke with confidence and authority. His expression darkened after a moment. "Really? Okay, I'll tell him." He hung up.

"It's about me, sir?" I asked, a little worried. I pulled at the tether connecting me to Rachel and felt her happy. She was singing and the sound made me smile. It wasn't her, thank goodness.

"It's Malefactor. He's asking you to come and help him gather some info." I tried my best not to look annoyed, but the expression spread across my face faster than I could control it. Shane laughed at me.

"What, he doesn't look young enough to interest the girls?" I asked, a little sarcastic. The last time Adam called me in under his undercover name, I ended up having to explain to Rachel why my pockets were stuffed with phone numbers.

I have to explain this, so hang on a moment. Remember when I said my DNA merged with a plant? It gave me a really weird ability once I reached puberty. For one, my eyes have an underlying glow to them. We called this my 'bioluminescence.' Basically, I attract people to me in an awkwardly sexual way. This makes me uncomfortable because I'm not used to so much attention, and the major fact that my heart already belongs to Rachel.

This ability, while annoying, can be hidden as long as I avoid eye contact by wearing a hood or something. Adam, however, likes to take advantage of it when he's trying to get information. Usually, because certain people are attracted to me because of my glow, all I have to do is occupy a corner somewhere and talk to people.

It sounds easy enough, but I'm an introvert, and crowds tend to make me nervous. It's part of my job, though, and when I'm called in, I have to suck it up. The information we find from these kinds of raids are usually what we need to infiltrate or take down the organization known as Uriel, which was tied to Ghost's Army.

These guys spell serious trouble. It was thanks to them that last year happened, and I'm sure if they could, they'd attempt to kill anyone associated with ANGEL.

Adam, although he was thirty-eight, still looked exactly the same as he did when he was twenty. We could have probably passed for buddies in school, which I was sure would annoy Adam to no end if he heard me say that. It had to do with his *regener*.

"You're a little more in the know about whatever kids find relevant these days," Shane tried to encourage me. I rolled my eyes.

"Not sure you really want to know what's considered relevant, sir," I joked and Shane smiled.

"I could tell you some stories, kiddo, but you're dating my daughter and I'm not really keen on giving you ideas. Remember, whatever sick, twisted little thoughts you boys can come up with, I did them first." He gave me a severe glance that sent shivers down my spine. It made me pretty positive that he was warning me not to try anything with Rachel. I wondered if he would consider my sneaking into her room late at night as 'trying something.'

"All right, where am I going?" I asked, changing the subject. Shane's look told me that he had plans to give me a talk. I found myself fervently wishing Rachel would hurry and grow up.

"The usual place," Shane replied, his voice oddly detached. I swallowed, finding Shane intimidating. I remembered him from my earliest of memories as being the kind of man who lived up to his promises... or threats.

"Let go of me, Sherlock. I have work to do," I sighed and Sherlock hesitantly detached himself from me. I offered my friend a smile before I left, hoping that it would make him happy enough to smile. Like any man's best friend, Sherlock had the sad puppy face down, and it always bothered me when he made that face at me when I left.

He smiled at me and 'wagged' as I turned and made my way to the teen club where most of Ghost's Army's Rogues hung out.

∞

Adam was waiting for me with his usual annoyed stance, girls young enough to be his daughter practically crawling all over him for his attention and stuffing numbers into his pockets. His expression took on a slightly relieved tone when he spotted me and his lip curled up into a smirk.

"My friend's here, ladies, so I've gotta go," he said and approached me. He slicked back his hair and gritted his teeth when he was in earshot of only me. "Took you long enough," he growled, popping a cigarette into his mouth.

I had always found that habit disgusting, but Adam picked it up when it became apparent that his marriage with Michal had failed beyond repair. He always felt guilty about it, not that he would ever tell anyone that, even though it was painfully obvious to those who knew him.

"Yeah, sorry. Sherlock had a hard time letting me go," I explained.

"He should have come, we could have used him," Adam said, looking around at the girls that outnumbered us.

My eyes flicked over to movement I'd spotted since I got out of my car and I smirked.

"If that's the case... hey, Sherlock! I can see you, you damn dog!" I called.

Sherlock must have followed me because he came out from behind the building, looking guilty. I smiled gently, amused.

"I'm sorry, boss. I was worried and thought maybe I ought to keep an eye on you," he muttered, unable to make eye contact. I tagged his arm as he came within reach and offered him an encouraging smile.

"Well, I'm glad you came because we could really use your help here. There's too many of them and too few of us. Can you help us out?" I asked. Sherlock grinned, his larger than normal canines giving him the look of a goth. I knew those fangs were real, though, and had seen them in action.

"Sure thing, boss," he said and Adam cleared his throat.

"Well, if you two girls are done braiding each other's hair, shall we?" Adam said, obviously annoyed.

Sherlock bounced alongside me as we walked into the establishment. The bar consisted of several pool tables, an obnoxiously loud jukebox, and non-alcoholic drinks that seemed to obtain a certain bite after hours.

Today, it was filled with kids my own age betting on pool and talking all sorts of nonsense to sound cooler than their buddies. I found this attitude to be obnoxious and I almost always left this place feeling drained and irritable.

Adam took up his usual position at the bar, a sick grin on his face. I could only imagine where he learned that expression, but I didn't say anything and tapped Sherlock's shoulder hard enough that he audibly woofed and wagged slowly, hunching his shoulders as if he was scared or uncomfortable.

His instincts were dead on, of course. This was the kind of place I wished fervently to never find Rachel or any girl I knew in, and if I didn't have to be there myself, I'd never step foot in a place that was obviously designed to trap kids into a certain lifestyle.

All I had to do was stand next to the jukebox and flash my gray eyes around the room before people suddenly began to gather around me.

"Your scar is really cool," a girl with chestnut hair and hazel eyes said to me as an opener. I wondered if her style of dress was comfortable considering how tightly her clothing clung to her body.

I couldn't help but stare, truth be told. I found myself imagining how I'd feel if Rachel dressed in such revealing clothing and had to turn my head away. I crossed my arms, trying not to look as annoyed as I felt.

Of course, that aloofness was what interested the girl even more. She was joined by another girl with hair so damaged from bleaching that it looked like she'd stuck her finger in a light socket.

"You're really hot, if you don't mind my saying so," the blonde girl said, her round blue eyes trained on me lustfully. I gave her one of my trademarked side glances and watched her face turn red.

I would never understand girls.

"It's a free country." I replied with the most blasé thing I could think of.

"God, can I just... I'd really love to fuck you," she said, practically pushing her friend out of the way.

"Trish!" the girl hissed. Trish, the blonde, wrapped her arms around my waist and pressed her body to mine.

In my defense, my brain told me someone wanted to play, not that I was actually aroused or attracted to this girl. The awkward moment lasted seconds, but was enough to embarrass me to the point of pushing the girl away a little.

"Do you always throw yourself at guys?" I asked as she looked up at me in shock. Clearly, this girl wasn't used to hearing the word no.

"When he's as hot as you. You simply ooze sex, doesn't he, Taylor?" I looked at the other girl who bit her lip in anger.

"Hey, easy girls. There's plenty of me to go around." I hated myself so much, I wanted to punch myself. This was a side of me that I did *not* want Rachel to ever see.

Taylor hesitantly leaned into my other side and I led the girls into one of the corner booths, sitting down with one arm draped around each girl.

Trish hooked her leg over mine and put her hand on my chest, which made my skin crawl. Necessary evils and all that.

"So, you want to rent the upstairs room?" Trish asked. I stared at her blankly for a moment.

"You can rent a room?" I asked, finding the comment interesting.

"By the hour," Taylor answered, sounding detached. Trish's hand moved from my chest down to my stomach. I felt sick because I knew what she was doing and it was grossing me out.

"My buddy was telling me about a certain program in this place... do you know about it?" I asked, stretching out my legs.

That was when Trish stuck her hand down the front of my pants. I didn't remember moving, but I was suddenly on the other side of Taylor and my eyebrows were raised at Trish.

She giggled and put her hand up to her lips. It took all of my willpower not to sneer at her.

"Why so shy, big man?" she asked.

Memories flashed around in my head in such rapid succession that I had to shake my head. "I don't like being violated," I growled dangerously. The color in Trish's face drained.

"I-I didn't mean...."

"I never said I wanted to sleep with you!" I growled forcefully.

"I can show you what the program is," Taylor said, suddenly in a better mood.

"Do you want to touch my dick, too?" I asked, the threat in my voice obvious.

Sherlock suddenly jumped on my back and I staggered a little before I found my footing.

"Which one of you girls pissed my homeboy off?" he asked, practically climbing of top of me.

"Hey, heel, you goddamn mutt!" I muttered, and when Sherlock laughed at my usual greeting, I felt a bit calmer.

"I claim the blondie! She's pretty cute!" Sherlock said, pushing on my shoulders and stretching out his torso, like I was some kind of rock he conquered. I jerked myself forward and Sherlock tumbled over my shoulders and landed in Taylor's lap head first.

I laughed as Sherlock grinned at Taylor and Trish.

"I wanted your buddy," Trish pouted, crossing her arms.

"He's got a girlfriend," Sherlock said with a shrug. I opened my mouth in disbelief at Sherlock's nonchalant response. "He also doesn't like it when a girl touches him without his express permission." Sherlock then leaned in conspiratorially and whispered, "He's got baggage."

"You stupid dog!" I cried in mock horror. Secretly, I was completely relieved for Sherlock's presence. I pulled Sherlock off of Taylor's lap and put him in a headlock.

"Thanks," I whispered to him.

"You're the stupid one!" Sherlock cried, yelping and trying to pull away. But he looked up at me a grinned. "You've got such a sweet girl at home, and you got me. If you're that hard up...."

I covered his mouth with my hand and Sherlock barked a laugh and pulled out of my headlock.

"You're a sick puppy!" I growled playfully at my friend. He grinned at me.

"Don't I know it," he replied and flung himself into the spot where I had been. Trish suddenly got up, her hands balled up at her sides. She looked angry, and I wondered if she was angry that I wasn't paying her any attention when she tackled me. I felt her grab something from my pocket before she ran off.

I stood and realized with icy panic that she had taken my present to Rachel from my jacket pocket. I took off after her and had Sherlock right on my heels as I yelled, "Give that back!" I stopped mid-room and crouched, activating my black *Auros* with an unnecessary incantation of 'Lights Out.'

My *Auros* was considered rare in that I could create a radius that temporarily disconnected other Chosen from their *Auros*. It had only two blind spots, the first of which was that it didn't affect any *Auros* that worked inside the body, like Adam's *regener* or Sherlock's dog-like sense of smell. The second power it didn't affect was anything having to do with telepathy. I never could figure out why that was.

Dodging through a rowdy crowd of teenagers is definitely a feat when you're six foot three and lanky, trying to tail a girl about five foot four and skinny. Never mind the occasional guy who thought I was chasing after her for all the wrong reasons and attempted to trip me up or stop me.

One guy attempted to clothesline me, but I somersaulted under his arm and came back to my feet in a graceful arc without losing much momentum.

Unfortunately, Sherlock got the clothesline instead and fell back with a sharp yelp of canine surprise, getting Adam's attention.

By this time, Trish was out of the bar and in the street, screaming the whole time that I was going to kill her and for someone to please help her.

I hated it when girls did that. She sprinted for the park and I boosted my speed. She may have been smaller, but I had endurance and training. I tackled her in the grass and watched as the box opened and the ring flew out into the grass in horrifying slow motion.

"Why the hell did you do that?!" I screamed at her, handcuffing her and picking up the empty box. I began to gently comb through the grass, but I hadn't seen where the ring landed. My heart sank. There was no way I going to find the ring in such tall grass right by tree roots.

"I wanted to teach you a lesson! Looks like it worked. You'll never ignore me again!" she said with a sadistic laugh.

That ring had been custom made. It took me months of paperwork and waiting just to have the damn thing approved because it was special. It was ANGEL's Bio Ring, which was required to be worn by all ARCs. It would take me another few months just to get it replaced, and the thought made my heart sink.

I trembled with disbelief. Why had I waited to give it to her? I stood and tossed the box at the girl. It hit her arm and she cried out as it bounced and hit her in her smug little face. I took off the cuffs and pushed her into the grass with my foot.

"Get the fuck out of here before I change my mind," I growled at her. She didn't need to be told twice, a little red welt appearing where I hit her with the box. Sherlock came skidding to a halt beside me and took my arm in his large hands.

"What happened?"

I sighed in anguish.

"I lost the ring I was going to give Rachel because of that bitch!" I cried, frustrated. "And I got nothing to report to Adam, which makes today a total waste!"

Sherlock frowned and I handed him the empty box. "Tell Adam I didn't get anything. I'm going home."

Sherlock whined softly as I walked away, and he was still sitting in the grass when I got in my car and drove away.

Rachel's Gift

I sighed as Charlie frowned at me.

"I'm sorry, kiddo, I really am. That ring was truly crafted from the heart, but a replacement, even if I rushed it, would take at least a month. There's no way I can get it to you in time for Rachel's party on the 23rd, much less in time for Christmas," Charles Grayson said. Charlie was ANGEL hospital's prominent doctor and was in charge of keeping an eye on the Bio Rings and Bands. He also happened to be an old friend of not just mine, but also my father and the Graham family.

I sighed again and closed my eyes. I still couldn't believe that someone had stolen that ring from me and then promptly lost it in the grass at Acacia-freaking-Park, the site of one of the bloodiest Chosen battles in our short history.

"Why don't you get her something else this year?" Charlie suggested. I sighed exaggeratedly and tried not to roll my eyes.

"I almost died on her last year. I really wanted to make this year special," I tried to explain. I didn't even know if those words truly covered how I felt about the whole thing. Rachel was so integral to who I was, I didn't want to just give her anything. I wanted to promise her all of me, and not just any ring would do. That ring was made of rose gold with tiny rose gold flowers containing our birthstones welded to the band around a princess cut diamond in the center and a vine pattern carved into the band itself.

That ring, because of the technology involved, had cost a small fortune, but saving money that I'd been paid since I was six had helped. She was worth every penny. Not that I still didn't have quite a bit in my savings, but it was what that ring symbolized. Somehow that little band spoke volumes about my love, admiration, and the promise that I wasn't going anywhere.

Not a single thing could replace that, and it angered me and made me sad all at once.

"I... I understand," I said dejectedly after Charlie struggled with what to tell me.

"Don't worry, Timothy. She'll understand," Charlie tried to reassure me.

"Maybe she will, but she won't know what it meant to me," I said and opened the door of his office only to almost get bowled over by Sherlock. He looked surprised to see me.

"Oh, hey, Tim—"

"I'll see you later, Sherlie." I sighed and passed my friend, who looked conflicted, but then shrugged and entered Charlie's office, closing the door behind him.

∞

Rachel was curled up on the couch next to the fire when I got home. Her hair was neatly tucked over one shoulder in a loose braid. She had a book in her lap and wore a long tunic shirt over gray leggings and baggy knee-high socks. The tunic hung off of one shoulder and the royal blue strap of her tank top was visible. The color of her tank top contrasted beautifully with her pale, freckled skin, and wisps of curly red hair sticking out here and there from her braid.

She was really becoming quite a woman, and I admired her almost hungrily. She was so beautiful with the orange light from the fire gently flickering across her silhouette that it made my heart ache. How could I have lost something so precious? Rachel and I had been through so much together, why did stuff keep happening to us?

She looked up at me, her face perplexed and her eyes that rare indigo they turned whenever she was using her *Auros*.

"Hey," I said softly, my voice deep and quiet.

"Hey," she replied, smiling encouragingly. I sat down next to her, careful not to touch her. She preferred a little space when she read.

Which is probably why I was shocked when she leaned back into my shoulder and looked up at me, her beautiful mismatched eyes gazing lovingly into mine.

"What happened to you? Your heart is so heavy," she said, closing the book and putting her arms around my shoulders. I exhaled and breathed in her scent, a tender mix of lilacs, roses, and a hint of vanilla. It had been my favorite scent since I was ten and didn't know how to handle an adoring five-year-old girl who thought I was 'the most beautiful boy' she'd ever seen.

I'm not sure how it happened, but I was suddenly kissing her deeply, our tongues caressing each other. She pulled away first, apparently feeling a little over-stimulated and breathless.

"Tim...." she breathed my name. She was the only one who could get away with calling me that.

"I love you," I replied, as if that was the perfect excuse. She smiled, her eyes dancing as she tried to gaze at both of my eyes at once. I touched her cheek, absolutely in love with the girl, and she smiled, her cheeks glowing red in the firelight.

"I love you, too, but you aren't answering my question," she said after clearing her throat.

"I just... I lost something important to me today," I explained.

"What was it?" she asked, frowning.

"Nothing that important. I'm with you now," I explained, holding her and putting my head in the small space between her developing breasts. She held my head there and I could hear her heart beating, which was soothing despite what I had lost.

"I'm not buying it, but if you don't want to talk about it, I won't press," she said, her voice a tender melody to my heart-sick ears. She was so sweet. The only girl who saw me as a real human being, despite all indicators to the contrary. By the time I had realized I was in love with her, it seemed like I'd loved her since I was a little boy gazing into mismatched eyes and playing hide and seek.

"What do you want for Christmas?" I asked her. She looked down at me, separating my head from her chest so she could gaze into my eyes. Her gaze was a little hard, like she couldn't believe I had asked that. "I'm being serious," I added.

"I have what I want. You're here. You live here with me, and I get to see you every day. I love you, and I need you."

"I'm so sorry that I almost—" I began, my voice cracking a little, but she hushed me.

"Don't say it," she whispered. "Timothy, I don't want anything physical, I just want you physically."

I smiled at that, fully knowing that she hadn't meant it the way it had sounded and watching her blush as she realized what she had said.

"*With* me, Timothy! God, you're such a perv!" she cried, playfully hitting my shoulder.

I laughed, pulling her toward me so I could kiss her again. "You always know how to make me feel so much better," I whispered to her.

Her eyes were closed as she savored the kiss, and she reveled in the feeling for moment before she breathlessly replied, "It's not like I say those things on purpose."

"Hurry and grow the fuck up, then," I encouraged her. She looked down at me and grinned before sliding off of my lap and the couch.

"I've got homework to do tonight, so...." I grinned, followed her into the kitchen, and sat down with her, holding her left hand as she did her homework and guiding her whenever she needed it.

∞

Work was its usual draggy thing, with the exception that Sherlock was a little more annoying than usual. He was, if you'll pardon the expression, dogging me as often as he could, so I had to find ways to give him the slip if I wanted to remember how to breathe.

I knew the dog meant well, but he was so excited about something and felt that he couldn't tell me, so I assumed it had something to do with the Christmas party and a gift he'd apparently gotten me.

I didn't much care, honestly, but Sherlock was excited as hell and it was hard not to find his enthusiasm infectious. The day of the party came upon us, and almost as if on cue, snow began to fall just as it had on Christmas Eve last year. I think that made Rachel jumpy because she was constantly texting me.

I texted her back to let her know I was fine and to tell her to stop worrying, but the stress she was feeling found its way into our tether and I felt it as keenly as if it were my own. No words could make her feel any better. She kept remembering things she shouldn't have, like images of blood on the snow and being so cold that she was numb, too terrified to think of anything else as I struggled for breath in her arms.

I was sitting in the locker room with an open box on my knee, staring at the plain-looking ID bracelet I'd purchased on a whim. I'd had it engraved and was able to pick it up just this morning.

'*Fioriture Eternita Attraverso Il Nostro Amore,*' followed by, 'TAG + RMG.' It was so lame. Rachel's father, Shane, was always warbling to her in Italian, so I thought I'd try to be poetic. 'Eternity blooms through our love.' I thought it was incredibly stupid, but what else could I do? I'd lost the real symbol of my love. Maybe this plain, inscribed rose gold bracelet would somehow get that message across.

That was when Adam came over. I hadn't noticed him watching me until he plopped down on the bench next to me. I looked over at him, grasping the bracelet before it fell, but Adam had it before I could grab it. He examined it, holding it up to the light. It was hard to imagine him as Rachel's father because he looked so young.

"Fee... fee or ray... E... eter nee ta... what is this gibberish? It sounds Italian," he said, handing the bracelet back and putting on one of his sneakers by placing his foot on the edge of the bench.

"It is," I said haltingly, still terrified of the man.

"Ah. My dumbass brother rubs off on everyone these days. He's the golden boy," Adam grumbled, switching feet. "Is that for my daughter?" he asked, his long hair falling over his shoulder.

"It is."

"What does it say?" he asked, as if conversationally. I didn't want to tell him.

"It's... incredibly stupid, sir. I'd rather not—"

"It's not inappropriate, is it, Timothy?" Adam asked, eyeing me like I was a stain on his favorite t-shirt.

I didn't flinch in the face of his scrutiny and I sighed, pulling my suit jacket on and tying my tie, a deep indigo color like her eyes when she used her *Auros*. After I was sure my tie was on straight, I stepped into my dress shoes and looked at myself in the mirror. I was always somewhat disappointed with what I saw there. In the ugly fluorescent light of the locker room, my skin looked horribly gray, the scar on my cheek only slightly obscured by a long piece of silvery white hair that fell over my forehead. My eyes were a strange long, rhombus shape, but were as wide as they were narrow, housing cold, gray eyes that held a strange silver glow. My eyebrows were thick and black, just like my impossibly long eyelashes. I was tall and skinny, despite all the muscles I had developed. My hair was cut weird, some pieces long and others short. I was emo and goth-looking all at once.

She thought the world of me, but I didn't think much of myself. I was never taught to think of myself as anything other than a tool for keeping the peace and being a protector. Why did a beautiful girl like Rachel fall in love with a guy like me?

"Timothy?" Adam asked, pulling me out of my reverie with an impatient tone.

"Oh, of course not. It's something I Google translated. It probably doesn't even mean what I think it means. It's meant to be... l-loving...." the last part came out as a barely audible whisper, I was so embarrassed.

"What does it mean, Timothy?"

At this point, I was annoyed and I looked Adam straight in the eye as I said, "That I love her."

Adam seemed taken aback by my attitude but smiled after a moment as if pleased with my answer.

"I'm pretty sure she'll like whatever you give her, Timothy. I was just wondering why you were looking at it as if it were offensive and not a pretty bauble for the girl you love."

I opened my mouth to speak, but then stopped myself. I knew Adam would not take kindly to a ring given by a young man of eighteen to his thirteen-year-old girlfriend, no matter how strongly bonded we were. Rachel's age was always a problem, and one of the reasons why it took me so long to confess to her.

He just wouldn't understand. I sighed and shook my head. "It's really nothing. I just hope she doesn't think it's stupid."

"I doubt it," Adam said with a pleasant smile on his face.

"Adam?" I called after him as he stepped away. He turned around and looked at me, his expression pleasant enough.

"Did you know?" I asked him, swallowing against my nerves.

"Did I know what?" he asked, facing me.

My blood rushed in my veins so fast, I was surprised no one could hear my heart beating. I was terrified to ask him, but I knew I had to.

"Um, one year ago... Adam, did you know that my blood type was B-negative?"

Adam stared at me, and after a moment, his face became white and his eyes widened.

"No, I didn't... Timothy, please tell me that I—" he said, rushing up to me and grabbing my shoulders. He was using his healing *Auros* to read my body, but I knew he wouldn't find what he was looking for.

"It's not going to be there. I absorbed it and it's now mine. You gave me a new ability when you saved my life," I explained.

Adam hugged me, his whole body trembling.

"I'm sorry," he whispered.

"I haven't told anyone else yet, just you," I said, a little alarmed that Adam was hugging me.

"I didn't tell anyone what I did to save your life, strictly because it was forbidden," Adam said, pulling away from me and looking at me. In his dark blue eyes was the true indication of his age, wise and sad.

I nodded. "I know. You sacrificed a lot to save me."

"Are you going to be worth it, I wonder?" Adam asked, gazing at me like a father gauging his child, as if he could somehow be certain of my worth just by his scrutiny. I offered him a little smile for his efforts. As much as the man scared me, I realized that he was just as much looking out for me as he was disapproving of my relationship with his daughter.

"I would hope so, sir," I said and played with my hair, trying to make sure it lay right. Adam smiled, which was rare, and mussed up my hair. As I protested, he laughed softly, grabbed his jacket, and left.

I found myself admiring him, unable to help myself. Adam Graham was certainly an interesting and complex man.

∞

The party was held in a hall, carefully decorated to look like an old ballroom. One side of the room housed food and refreshments, and in one of the corners stood a beautiful Christmas tree with a mountain of presents at the bottom.

The Graham family greeted the guests enthusiastically. Shane had his arm around his wife, who seemed like she was glowing. Next to her was Abel, who seemed nervous for some reason, and Isaac, who held a notebook and pen and seemed to be working on math problems between greetings. Rachel looked absolutely beautiful, her hair curled into perfect cascades and shining with golden highlights, her party dress a beautiful crimson color. Next to her were her sisters, Charlie and Raye, both of them with shining curls framing their faces, and the baby of the family, Shane Adam, looking bored out of his young little skull, a spitting image of his father with the exception of his hazel eyes and dark auburn hair.

"Timothy, our guest of honor!" Shane jovially called out to me. I weakly smiled at him, a little embarrassed by the attention. I waved to be polite and Shane stepped forward, shaking my hand.

"So, the girls—" Shane began, but was interrupted by bouncing little girls too excited to stand still.

"Dance with me, Timothy, please?" Raye asked, her golden curls bouncing around her face like a doll's. Charlie was suddenly at my side, holding me by my elbow.

"No, with me!" she pouted. I looked up at Rachel, who smiled in amusement at her younger siblings. She came over and kissed me, standing on her tip-toes to whisper into my ear.

"My sisters apparently have been harboring little crushes on you. You wouldn't mind giving them a dance or two? I still need to wrap your present anyway," she whispered, her breath hot on my ear. I swallowed against the feelings it stirred up in me.

"I thought you were my present... look at that packaging," I playfully whispered back. She smiled, her feelings reflecting my own. She looked so grown up suddenly.

"I'll see you in a little bit," she said and walked away. I would have watched her walk away if it hadn't been for her sisters tugging me and making me aware of their presence again.

"I want to!" Raye was shouting at Charlie, who only trembled, her lips in a tight frown.

"Girls, I'll dance with both of you. Charlie, would you mind if danced with Raye first?" I asked the younger girl. She looked up at me, her eyes widening. I smiled at her and she slowly let go of my arm. She walked dejectedly to her mother and I caught her crying as Michal held her and spoke soothingly to her. I felt bad that I'd made Charlie cry, but I was certain I had a way to make it up to her.

I brought Raye over to the dance floor and she slipped out of her flat shoes, stepping on my feet as I swirled her around the dance floor while she laughed and told me funny stories about her day. When the song ended, I gave Raye a hug before she traipsed off toward the food. I spotted Charlie across the room, still upset, and looked all around me for something special. I spotted it and grabbed the flower from a nearby display, swooping in as charmingly as I could and placing the large white peony into Charlie's hair. Her eyes widened and she gasped as I picked her up.

"Are you ready to dance, Princess?" I asked her, tucking her brown hair behind her ear. I brought her out to the dance floor as her young face turned red. She didn't say anything as I danced with her, but she stared at me as if trying to commit everything about our dance to memory. At the end of our dance, I brought her over to the edge of the dance floor and knelt before her, encouraging her to sit on my knee.

She shyly obliged, looking up at me with an expression I was familiar with because her older sister showered me with it frequently. I thought it was cute that Charlie had crush on me, so I wanted to show her the kind of man I thought she should be encouraged to find later. Someone who would show her respect and love her deeply.

I smiled at her and produced a gift box from my pocket. When I put it in her young hands, her eyes widened and tears misted them. She opened the box to find the Tiffany chain bracelet I'd gotten for her.

"You really want to give *me* this? Not Rachel?" she asked, her voice tight. I smiled and kissed her forehead.

"No. This present is for you, Charlotte. I wanted you to know that I'm here for you and your sisters. I've decided you're always going to be my little princess. Sadly, my heart belongs to Rachel."

"I know that," she replied, her voice tiny and a little sad, but she looked up at me, touching her forehead where I had kissed her. "But... I'm always your little princess?" she asked, her voice quiet.

"Yup. Only Lotte Graham," I replied. She threw her tiny arms around my neck and kissed my cheek.

"I'll treasure this always, Timothy," she whispered and let me clasp it to her wrist. She hugged me again before sliding off of my knee and running up to Rachel to show her the heart charm on the bracelet. I smiled when Rachel looked over at me with a smile. I then sighed when I thought of what I had for the love of my life.

So lame.

"Timothy!" came a familiar bark from across the room. I winced and turned just as my best friend knocked me over. "I got a present for ya!" he said as he helped me back to my feet.

"I'm not really in the mood, mutt," I sighed, closing my eyes.

"Timothy!" Raye came over suddenly, and she seemed a little mad. It made me smile a little because I knew she thought I'd forgotten about her.

"Did you really just—" she began, as fiery as her *Auros*. I interrupted her with a box of her own, tapping it to her forehead. She gasped and then squealed in delight, opening it.

I had gotten Raye a teardrop necklace in which the jewel looked much like a flame, the edges being white and transitioning into a warm pinkish orange, and then into a deep sapphire blue.

"Oh, my God!" she cried and hugged me so hard that I lost air for a moment.

"You're welcome," I chuckled, patting her head. I shook my head as I watched her sprint off toward her parents, showing off her new treasure. I turned my attention to Sherlock and he smirked at me, which always made me nervous.

"Trying to show off to your girl? They say the quickest way to a girl's heart is to get her sister's seal of approval."

"Like I need to bribe Rachel's sisters to get her heart," I commented drily.

"You could use jewelry, but how are you going to top off a tourmaline stone and a Tiffany bracelet?" I felt a little ashamed by Sherlock's teasing, but my instincts were going crazy. Something was definitely up.

"Please don't tell me you're going to give me jewelry," I said nervously. Sherlock barked a laugh and flung something at me. I caught it and opened the long, rectangular box to find a tactical pen. It was sharp-looking with a glass breaker on the end. It twisted off at about the middle to reveal a small, serrated knife and the clip doubled as a seatbelt cutter.

"Damn." I whistled, unable to say anything as I looked up at my friend. He was still grinning at me.

"Look inside the box, bro," he said. Curious, I put the pen in my pocket, peered into the box, and found something floating in there. When I shook it out, my jaw dropped.

There was my ring! It looked pristine and perfect, like it had been recently cleaned. I smiled and hugged my friend, who laughed and kissed my cheek.

"Where did you find it?" I asked.

"In the grass, bro. I have an excellent sense of smell, if you recall. It was nothing for me to sniff around the grass for a bit to find it for you. You seemed so broken-hearted, I figured it was all I could do to help you feel better. Now you can give your sweetheart her real gift."

"Thanks, Sherlie. I owe you one," I said, still awed.

"Just one?" he asked, 'wagging' and smiling at me. I left him with a pat to my lapel to show him how much I appreciated the gift.

"You can find your gift under the tree, Sherlock. And really, man. Thanks," I said and watched Sherlock practically sprint to the tree and, with a few sniffs, find his gift. I smiled, shaking my head and turning to find Rachel.

I found her on the other side of the room like she'd been waiting for me. I kissed her once I was in range, and to my surprise, she kissed me back passionately.

"What was that for?"

"Making my sisters happy. I hope you brought something for everyone, or Abel is gonna be pissed," she joked. I smiled, in love with her all over again.

"Got him a game. I got Isaac a gift certificate to get whatever text books he wants, and I even got a little puzzle game for Shane Adam."

"That's my man," Rachel said, which made me blush. A man. She saw me as an adult. That made me really happy and scared all at once.

"Rachel... um, I actually have two presents for you. One of them was sort of a backup gift because I—"

"I don't need an explanation, Timothy. I have a present for you, too, love," she said, holding a square box in her hands.

I fished in my pocket for the ID bracelet and held it out to her. Her eyes widened and she gently touched it, fingering the little heart charm that hung on it.

"Oh, Timothy... it's so beautiful!" she gasped. I smiled as I put it on her wrist and watched her admire it.

"I'm sorry if the Italian isn't right," I said.

"It's fine. Thank you, Timo—"

"I'm not done, Rachel," I said, taking her hand and leading her over to a corner where we could have a little more privacy. She looked up at me, her mismatched eyes dancing in the glow of the room.

"I love you so much that I almost gave up my life to save yours last year and I don't ever want to put you through that again. I can't," I said, trying to emphasize what I meant. Rachel looked at me with a slight tilt of her head as I knelt before her. "I hereby pledge myself, body, mind, and soul to you, Rachel Marian Graham," I said, holding up the ring.

I was such a nervous wreck, I wondered if what I said was actually what ended up coming out of my mouth because of the confused look Rachel gave me.

"Are... are you promising yourself to me?" she asked quietly. I looked up at her, scared and confused and determined all at once.

"I'm asking you, Rach, if you'll do the same. I know you're young, but—" I didn't get to finish as Rachel threw herself into my arms and almost knocked me over.

"You've never had to ask, Timothy!" Rachel sobbed. I stroked her back.

"But I feel so... responsible for your fear and doubts and I... I guess I was just hoping—"

"That proposing to me would make me feel at ease?" she finished for me.

My shoulders slumped as I realized how lame I was. Maybe the only person I was trying to convince was myself.

"You've always had my heart," she said and kissed me.

She held out her hand to me and I slipped the ring on her finger as I kissed her.

"I love you," I pledged.

"Thank you," she said. Her kiss tasted like her tears.

I stood after a moment and she pulled me back, handing me the box. I raised my eyebrows in surprise until I opened the box and found a thick, silver bracelet with the words, 'Never do we part. I love you, Tim. RMG.'

She clicked the cuff onto my left wrist and I stared at her before slowly smiling.

"I guess you wanted to mark me as yours, too, huh?" I asked her. She laughed and I pulled her out onto the dance floor where every song played was a slow dance to our ears. After Rachel became tired, I held her all night long until she eventually fell asleep, her arms around me and her head in the hollow of my shoulder.

I carried her home that night and lay her down in her bed, tugging off my tie and having left my wet shoes by the front door. Rachel looked up at me and I caught her gaze.

"Timothy... don't leave," she whispered.

It took me a moment to realize what she was actually saying and I held my breath.

Oh.

I turned around and opened the door before I climbed into bed with her, wrapping her up in my arms. I trembled with the feelings that swirled around in her head. The pain of the past eased, replaced by the warmth of my body, the promise of a long future together, and for her, it wasn't *enough*. If I truly wanted a future with her, I would have to spend every day convincing her that I wasn't going anywhere. That I would never leave her behind.

"I got the test results from Charlie back," I whispered to her.

"Test?" she asked.

"You never knew that Adam injected me with his *regener* to save my life. Did you know that Adam and I have the same blood type?"

Rachel froze and turned her head to look back at me.

"No," she said cautiously. I smiled at her.

"I've absorbed Adam's *regener*. I will probably never age, just like him, and I will never leave you again." I kissed her neck, nervous as hell for finally saying it, but at peace for having told her.

Rachel's initial panic faded fairly quickly, which impressed me.

"Oh," she said, and then began to cry, suddenly grateful to her father for a gift she never knew he gave.

I was half asleep when Adam found us together on her bed. I heard him sigh deeply and I pretended to be asleep, if for no other reason than to seem less threatening.

What surprised me was the feeling of a blanket covering me and a gentle touch to my forehead.

"Thank you so much, Daddy. For saving Timothy's life," Rachel whispered.

Adam's voice broke as he responded. "Anything for my girl."

"I love you, Papa Adam," Rachel sighed happily.

"I love you, too. Good night, baby girl," Adam replied, kissing her before leaving the room.

I'm not sure I ever felt so at peace as that night when Rachel accepted Adam as her father, Adam accepted me as being integral to Rachel, and I learned that, for as hard and cold as that man seemed, Adam was really just a concerned father, not just for Rachel....

But for me, too.

About the Author

Dalian Graylocke was born in Las Vegas, Nevada with seven 7's, three 3's, and one 21 in her birthday, making her a natural born performer. Aside from being a talented singer and songwriter, writing has always been a passion of hers. Check her out on soundcloud.com/tomikaiser or peruse her blog at daliangraylocke.weebly.com.

She lives in Washington State with her loving husband, doting brother, and adorable fur baby, Carmel.